NINE FOR CALIFORNIA

by Sonia Levitin

illustrated by Cat Bowman Smith

ORCHARD BOOKS
New York

For Lloyd with love —S.L.

In memory of my great-aunt, Frances
Bowman Yaw, who lived in a house of
sod in Dakota Territory during the days
of the stagecoach —C.B.S.

⟡

Thanks to Wells Fargo History Museum and Dr. Robert
Chandler, Wells Fargo Bank historian, for assistance and
information.

Orchard Books, A Grolier Company
95 Madison Avenue, New York, NY 10016

Manufactured in the United States of America
Printed and bound by Phoenix Color Corp.
Book design by Chris Hammill Paul

Hardcover 10 9 8 7 6 5
Paperback 10 9 8 7 6 5 4 3 2 1

The text of this book is set in 17 point Gloucester Old Style.
The illustrations are watercolor.

Library of Congress Cataloging-in-Publication Data
Levitin, Sonia, date.
Nine for California / by Sonia Levitin ; illustrated by
Cat Bowman Smith. p. cm.
Summary: Amanda travels by stagecoach with her four siblings and her
mother from Missouri to California to join her father.
ISBN 0-531-09527-4 (tr.)
ISBN 0-531-07176-6 (pbk.)
[1. Coaching—Fiction. 2. Frontier and pioneer life—
West (U.S.)— Fiction.] I. Smith, Cat Bowman, ill. II. Title.
PZ7.L58Ni 1996 [E]—dc20 96-1958

Pa sent a letter by stage. "Come to California, my dears. I am lonely without you." In the letter was a big bank note, all the money Pa had in the world. He had worked in the gold fields for a whole year. "What good is gold," Pa wrote, "without my family?"

Mama sent a letter back. "We're coming!" Then she bought a big sack and started to pack.

The neighbors said Mama was daft. "It's twenty-one days to Californ-y. Who would take five young'uns so far?"

"I would," said Mama. The sack grew fatter and fatter.

"What's in the sack, Mama?" I asked.

"Everything we'll need," Mama said.

"What will we need?" I asked.

"Wait and see," said Mama.

Everyone came to wave good-bye. People brought letters for their dear ones in far-off California.

Nine of us crowded into the stagecoach. Mr. Hooper, the banker, wore a tall black hat. Cowboy Charlie brought his lariat. Plump Miss Camilla, the teacher, sniffed at a little perfume bottle hanging from a chain around her neck.

Then there was Mama, Baby Betsy, Billy, Joe, Ted, and me — Amanda. The grown-ups looked at us with wide eyes. Their mouths drew in tight. Five children in that crowded little stagecoach for twenty-one days?

The stage driver stopped us, shouting, "Lady, put that sack on top with the other bags. It won't fit inside the stage!"

"Yes, it will," said Mama. "My girl Amanda will sit on the sack." And quick as a wink Mama hoisted her sack on board and I sat down on top of it. It felt all bumpy and lumpy, hard and soft. I was proud to be the one that Mama trusted.

We all sat so close that our knees knocked together, three facing forward, three backward, and three in the middle.

Six horses pulled at their reins, ready to run. The driver jumped onto the high seat. Beside him sat the shotgun rider with a gun on his shoulder.

"Hee-giddyap!" cried the driver. With a creak and a rumble, a heave and a shake, we were off. Trees and houses spun away. Dust flew into my eyes. My teeth rattled as we bounced and bumped and shook.

Baby Betsy screamed. "There, there," said Mama. "Hush, hush." Baby Betsy
threw up on Mr. Hooper's lap.

"Oh, dear-deary me. Amanda, get me a rag from the sack!"

I reached in and got Mama the rag. She mopped up the mess.

Mr. Hooper held his hat up high. Cowboy Charlie frowned over his lariat.
Miss Camilla sniffed her perfume bottle.

Baby Betsy got hiccups. Hic! Hic! Hic! It made
Billy giggle, then Joe, Ted, and me. We laughed our
giggle fits, rolling and punching one another.

Mr. Hooper grumbled to Mama, "My good woman, I hope you have
something in that sack to keep these children quiet. We have only just begun."
"Indeed," said Mama. From the sack she took a sugar lump for each of us.
We sucked and sucked, even Baby Betsy.

Brother Billy had brought his whistle. He began to toot. "Toot-tweet-toot," went the whistle. "Toot-tweet-toot."

Mr. Hooper twirled his hat. He told Mama, "My good woman, that whistle should have been left at home!"

Mama took the whistle and tucked it into the sack. "We'll see about that, Mr. Hooper," she said sweetly. From the sack Mama pulled a piece of string and started a cat's cradle. We leaned and we lurched all over one another, playing cat's cradle, I and my brothers, Billy, Joe, and Ted.

"Last stop in Missouri!" shouted the driver. "Next comes Kansas."

My legs felt curled up and wobbly. My stomach rolled over like the wooden wheels of the coach.

The stage driver brought a plate of beans for everyone, and a hunk of bread. Mama sat us all down in a row on a log. "Eat," she said.

"I hate beans," yelled my brothers.

"You'll like 'em by the time we get to Californ-y," said Mama. "Eat up."

"What's for dessert?" I asked Mama.

"Prunes," said Mama. "Amanda, go get them from the sack."

Back in the coach, my tummy felt funny, beans and prunes acting up. We giggled and gurgled. We made faces and noises.

Mr. Hooper glared at Mama and said, "My good woman, can't you find something better for your children to do?"

"Yes, indeed, Mr. Hooper," said Mama, and she called out, "Plants!"

Billy, Joe, Ted, and I named all the plants we knew. Then we named all the animals, all the birds, all the Presidents, the states in the union, and the oceans and countries of the world.

Mr. Hooper fanned himself with his hat. "My good woman," he said, "can't your children ever stop talking?"

"Stop talking, children," said Mama. "Let's sing."

We sang every song we knew. We sang in English, some in French, and we started over in pig Latin. Baby Betsy sang too, "Waa-waa-waa!"

Miss Camilla's face got very red. "Children should be seen and not heard," she said.

Night fell. "How much longer?" I asked Mama. "How much farther to go?"

"Only twenty days more," Mama said brightly. "Now go to sleep."

We slept in the stage, jostling and jiggling.

In the morning I felt all scrambled and sore. I looked out over the prairie, with endless grass and endless wind, and the long, long hours moaning by. I was so bored I thought I would die. All day I waited and hoped for something to happen.

It finally did.

We heard the pounding of horses
and terrible yells: "Yip! Yip! Yeeiow!"

"Indians!" shouted Cowboy
Charlie. The shotgun rider
drew his gun.

"Leave 'em be," said Mama.
"Those are Pawnee Indians,
friendly but hungry."

"We've got nothing to feed
them," said Mr. Hooper,
squeezing his hat in his hands.

Miss Camilla grew pale and
clutched her perfume bottle.

Mama pointed to the sack. I reached in and brought out a hunk of corn pone, enough for everyone. The Indians ate and smiled their thanks. Then they rode off.

"I'll be doggoned," gasped the driver.

We all got settled and started again.

Days dragged on. We counted minutes, hours, miles. It seemed that we had been traveling forever.

I yawned and groaned and wished that something would happen.

It did.

The sky went black. Jagged streaks of lightning crashed overhead. The horses shrieked and screamed. The coach pitched like a boat in the sea. Icy cold rain came down, a sudden flood. Hailstones the size of turkey's eggs pounded the coach.

"We're sinking in mud," called the driver. "Everyone out."

We climbed out into the freezing rain and the mud. Everyone heaved and pushed until the coach was unstuck.

Back inside the coach, we smelled like wet cats. Miss Camilla fluffed out her hair and touched the perfume to her curls. Mr. Hooper tried to reshape his hat. Cowboy Charlie wrung the water from his lariat. Everyone sighed. Baby Betsy cried.

Mama nodded toward the sack. "Nothing warms the bones like a hot licorice whip," said she. I reached in and gave licorice to everyone. Mr. Hooper, Cowboy Charlie, and Miss Camilla all smiled, and Miss Camilla's cheeks turned red.

The days dragged on. We ate beans and bread and prunes, and we liked them no better than we had at the start. The long road never ended. I wished that something would happen.

It did.

From far off we saw brown and shaggy beasts, like a huge dark stain on the fair prairie grasses.

"Buffalo!" shouted the driver. "Look out!" The shotgun rider turned and began to fire over the heads of the beasts.

Thousands of buffalo ran straight toward our coach. We heard them roar. We smelled their smell. The coach shook like a leaf in a storm.

Mama pulled the sack out from under me. "Pepper!" she cried.

I reached for a jar of red pepper and gave a handful to everyone, except for Baby Betsy. We leaned out the windows, ready. The buffalo came closer. I saw their flashing eyes.

"Now!" shouted Mama. I tossed my pepper right onto the nose of a huge
buffalo, the first one in the herd. It made the buffalo sneeze and snort. The
buffalo turned away and left our wagon standing, safe.

Days dragged on as before. Nothing changed but the sky, full of deep colors,
then stars. I wished something would happen.
It did.

The coach stopped. We fell forward.
Two men stood in the road. They wore masks.
They had pistols. One said, "Give us your gold,
your jewels, your silver."

Mama rounded her mouth and blew.
I reached into the sack for Billy's whistle.
I blew three hard, piercing blasts.

Startled, the robbers turned. The driver and the
shotgun rider and Cowboy Charlie jumped on
top of the outlaws. With his lariat Cowboy Charlie
tied the outlaws to a tree.

We all climbed back onto the coach.
We rode for days and days, nights and nights, up
mountains and down again, across rivers, into the endless dry desert.
I hoped and wished that something would happen.
   It did.

"Californ-y!" shouted the driver.

"Californ-y!" shouted everyone, except for Baby Betsy. She was finally asleep.

California! I could hardly believe it, I was so happy.

At the stagecoach stop about a million people came to greet us. One of them was my pa.

Pa waved his hat and cheered and smiled. He picked Mama right up and gave her a kiss. When he saw us five, Billy, Joe, Ted, Baby Betsy, and me, he kissed us all and swung us around, he was so glad.

Then Pa asked, "How was the trip? Anything happen?"

"Nothin' much," said Billy, Joe, Ted, and I. Mama only laughed.

Pa brought out our luggage, including the sack. Pa opened it and looked inside. He scratched his head. He smiled a crooked smile at Mama. "What a silly thing to do," he said, "bringing an empty sack from Missouri to Californ-y. I'm glad you've come to me, my dear. These children need someone with good sense to take care of them."

"Young'uns do need their pa, it's true," said Mama. She smiled at me and winked.

Mr. Hooper, the banker, took off his hat and gave Mama a little bow.

Cowboy Charlie laughed and laughed, his shoulders twitching, kind of quiet.

Miss Camilla, the teacher, gave Mama her little perfume bottle. "I'll never forget you," she said.

The three turned to Pa. "Nice family," said Mr. Hooper.

"Good young'uns," said Cowboy Charlie.

"Little ladies and gentlemen," said Miss Camilla.

Billy, Joe, Ted, and I kept our faces straight as we could, not daring to laugh.

Mama folded up the sack, and we headed for our new home.

When we were settled, Mama and I stuffed the sack with goose feathers. On winter nights we would lie on it, all five of us, sometimes Mama too, rocking and swaying, pretending we were in the stagecoach bound for California again.